# What Do Parents Do?

## (...when you're not home)

For Bob and "the boys"—Matt, Brian, and Alex
—J.F.R.

For Tracie, Joe, Joey, and Josh
—C.M.

Ω

Published by
PEACHTREE PUBLISHERS
1700 Chattahoochee Avenue
Atlanta, Georgia 30318-2112
www.peachtree-online.com

Text © 2007 by Jeanie Franz Ransom
Illustrations © 2007 by Cyd Moore

Book design by Cyd Moore
Art Direction by Loraine M. Joyner
Typesetting by Melanie McMahon Ives

Illustrations created in watercolor and colored pencil.

Printed in Malaysia
10 9 8 7 6 5 4 3 2

Library of Congress Cataloging-in-Publication Data

Ransom, Jeanie Franz, 1957-
    What do parents do when you're not home / written by Jeanie Franz Ransom ; illustrated by Cyd Moore. -- 1st ed.
        p. cm.
    Summary: While two children spend the night at Grandma's, their parents do all the things the children are forbid-
den from doing, like jump on the bed with their shoes on, dress up the dog, and get crumbs all over the bed sheets.
    ISBN 13: 978-1-56145-409-9 / ISBN 10: 1-56145-409-5
    [1. Parents--Fiction. 2. Behavior--Fiction. 3. Humorous stories.] I. Moore, Cyd, ill. II. Title.
    PZ7.R1744Wh 2007
    [E]--dc22
                                    2006024332

# What Do Parents Do?

## (...when you're not home)

Written by Jeanie Franz Ransom
Illustrated by Cyd Moore

Ω
PEACHTREE
ATLANTA

My little sister and I are spending the
night at our grandparents.

"Have fun," Mom says.

"We will!" says my sister.

"What are *you* going to do?" I ask.

"I'm sure we'll figure something out,"
Dad responds.

The minute we drive away, Mom and Dad run straight upstairs to their room and do exactly what they always tell us not to do...

Jump on the bed! With their shoes on.

Somebody *always* gets hurt when you play rough.

BERRIES
U-PIK

When they're tired of jumping
on the bed, Mom and Dad decide
to go sledding.
Even though that's not the way
we treat pillows in *our* house.

Mom and Dad watch TV for ages. They'll watch *anything*.
Even shows they've seen a bazillion times!

They sit way too close to the television.
Which is probably why they both wear glasses.

Mom and Dad get hungry, so they fix themselves a little snack. They've probably ruined their appetites. And they'd better hope those Kool-Aid stains come out!

After their snack, Mom and Dad run to the playroom and drag out all the toys. Mom goes *right* for my Beasty Bugs action figures. Dad wants to play with them, too. And nobody wants to take turns. You'd think by now they would have learned to share!

At least mom and dad can agree on *one* thing.
They both think it's a lot of fun to dress up the dog.

I don't know how the dog feels,
but those better not be clean clothes he's wearing!

Mom and Dad remember that they missed dinner. They grab some food and head into my room to play *my* video games!

They say they don't know how the games work, but I know better. They probably practice all the time when I'm not home.

Is that the best use of their time?

It's way past bedtime, but Mom and Dad aren't tired.
At least that's what *they* think.

They decide to play basketball, even though you're not supposed to play ball in the house!

After the ball goes out the window, Mom and Dad see who can get a dirty sock up on the ceiling fan first.

No wonder we can never find two socks that match!

Finally, they get ready for bed.

They don't even brush their teeth.

Mom and Dad stay up half the night reading comic books. They eat cookies—and get crumbs all over the clean sheets.

And don't tell me that dog is up on the bed again!

Eventually, Mom and Dad fall asleep.
They *have* to. We'll be home in the morning.

They've got a *lot* of work to do.
It looks like a tornado came through here!

When we come home the next morning,
I ask, "What did you do while we were gone?
"Oh, nothing much," Mom says.
"It's pretty quiet around here when you
two are gone," Dad adds.

"When did you say you're going to spend the night
with Grandma and Granddad again?" Mom asks.